This book belongs to

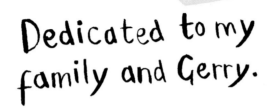

Dedicated to my family and Gerry.

A Dorling Kindersley Book

First published in Great Britain in 1998
by Dorling Kindersley Limited,
9 Henrietta Street, London WC2E 8PS

Visit us on the World Wide Web at http://www.dk.com

A CIP catalogue record for this book is available from the British Library.

ISBN 0 7513 7072 X (Hardback)
ISBN 0 7513 7184 X (Paperback)

Colour reproduction by Dot Gradations, UK
Printed in Hong Kong by Wing King Tong
2 4 6 8 10 9 7 5 3

I'm Too Busy

By Helen Stephens

It was a busy day in the city.

Charlie was directing traffic.

"I'm too busy for supper," said Charlie. "I'm directing traffic. Can't you see?"

"Hmmm.... what will tempt Charlie to eat his supper?"

"Look, Charlie," called Katy. "Fish soup!"

"I'm too busy for fish soup,"
said Charlie.
"I'm on the moon.
Can't you see?"

"I've made fishcakes, Charlie," said Katy. "Your favourite."

"Monsters don't eat fishcakes," Charlie growled.

"They eat elephants.
Ra!"

"There's jelly, too!"
called Katy.

"I'm too busy for jelly," said Charlie. "I'm dancing at the ball. Can't you see?"

"I can see," said Katy, "that you are too busy. Too busy for fish soup, fishcakes and jelly, too."

100 tonne wellies ↓

Charlie's
tummy
rumbled.

"Fish soup, fishcakes and jelly,"

Said Charlie.

"My favourites!"

And Katy smiled.

Other Toddler Books to collect—

PANDA BIG AND PANDA SMALL by Jane Cabrera

CATERPILLAR'S WISH by Mary Murphy

BABY LOVES by Michael Lawrence, Illustrated by Adrian Reynolds

THE PIG WHO WISHED by Joyce Dunbar, Illustrated by Selina Young